THE BIRD MAIDEN

To my mother, Marilyn McCrossen,
who always told me I could do it.

THE BIRD MAIDEN

A SERBIAN LEGEND

RETOLD BY JAN MIKE   ILLUSTRATED BY DAVE ALBERS

TROLL

 here once lived a king who had only one child, the young Prince Velimer. Servants granted the prince his every wish, tutors brought him the wonders of the world, and guardsmen protected him from danger. But the prince's mother had died when he was young, and his father was often busy with kingly matters. Prince Velimer was a lonely child who grew up to be a lonely man.

When it was time for the prince to marry, the king ordered three advisers to bring to the palace all eligible maidens from the neighboring kingdoms.

The first to arrive, with a battalion of guards and a bevy of maids, was the rich and beautiful Princess Roksanda. The king's advisers smiled as they admired her dowry of golden coins.

The prince and princess were ushered off to a state dinner. Prince Velimer watched as the princess amused herself by ordering servants back to the kitchen to fetch tidbits to satisfy her delicate appetite. Finally, a flustered maid spilled a cup of fresh berries on Princess Roksanda's white gown.

The princess squealed and slapped the girl's cheek. Furious, Prince Velimer stood and waved the sobbing maid out of the room. Then he left without a word.

The king's advisers hurried after him, speaking in their most soothing tones.

"It was merely a misunderstanding, young prince. Please remember that Princess Roksanda is *very* rich," the first adviser said.

"Mere girlish high spirits," the second adviser said. "Her father owns much land."

"She shows a proper queen's disposition," chimed in yet another adviser. "Your father will surely approve of this marriage."

"Send her away!" Prince Velimer said. "She tormented the servants and slapped the maid. I won't marry her."

The reluctant advisers pleaded with the prince, but he refused to change his mind.

Princess Roksanda was sent away, and the parade of eligible maidens continued. Princess Militza (who never bathed and couldn't add the simplest sums) was followed by Princess Iconia (who couldn't read and made her servants carry her everywhere), then Princess Elena (who never stopped talking and blew her nose on her sleeve).

Princess Elena had barely left the castle when the guards ushered in an apple-cheeked old woman. The woman knelt before the prince and sobbed into her apron.

"Help me, Prince Velimer."

"Help you do what, Grandmother?" Prince Velimer asked.

"Find my princess," the old woman answered. "I was Princess Yevrossima's nurse for many years. I swear that she is beautiful, kind, and clever. She healed her servants with herbs that she gathered, and she taught their children how to read."

Prince Velimer leaned forward, intrigued. "She sounds wonderful," he said. "Why has she not come to meet me?"

"Alas, she is gone! Last summer she went into the forest to gather medicines, and she never returned. Please help find her, Prince Velimer!"

The king's advisers yawned and polished their nails while the old woman spoke. As soon as she finished, they waved her off to the kitchen and escorted the prince to his room.

"Princess Yevrossima has very little money. I will send her nurse home tomorrow," the first adviser said as he fluffed the prince's pillows.

"Her father has almost no land," said the second adviser, sounding quite scandalized.

"Your father would never approve," said the third adviser, pursing his lips. "It is time for you to go to bed, your grace."

Without a word, the prince climbed into bed. As he lay awake, he thought about his life. He was tired of being ordered about like a child, and tired of being told whom to marry. Every princess he had met was vain and selfish. But Princess Yevrossima seemed different. Could she really be as wonderful as she sounded? He had to know.

hen his advisers were safely snoring, the prince rolled his jeweled dagger into a blanket. He sneaked down to the castle larder and filled a bag with food, then ran to the stable and saddled his horse. In the silver moonlight, he rode off, determined to find Princess Yevrossima.

Alone for the first time in his life, Prince Velimer soon discovered how helpless he was without any servants. There was no one to fix his meals or guard him while he slept. He persevered, and within a few weeks he had learned how to gather berries and nuts, to catch and cook fish, and to build a fire with rain-drenched wood.

Prince Velimer searched the forest where Princess Yevrossima had disappeared, but he saw no sign of her. As his muscles hardened and his hands grew calloused, he scoured the countryside day and night. Though the princess was nowhere to be found, Prince Velimer refused to give up.

One evening as he sat by a mountain stream, a golden lark swooped down and perched on his shoulder. Prince Velimer smiled and stroked the bird's soft wing.

"How can I help you, little bird?" he asked.

To his amazement, the bird answered.

"Rescue me, and you will be the happiest man in the world," the bird said.

"Rescue you?" asked the prince. "From whom?"

"On top of the mountain lives an old witch. She holds me under a powerful spell. Many men have tried to save me, but she turned them into boulders."

Prince Velimer touched the shivering bird. He hated to leave his search for the princess, but the little lark looked so sad.

"Tomorrow I will climb the mountain and free you from this witch," he said softly.

The golden lark gave a joyful trill, then tilted her head and looked Prince Velimer in the eye. "Each night, the old witch unbinds her hair. Grab on to it and hold it tight, no matter what she says or does, for she cannot enchant you while you hold her hair. Be careful. If she looks into your eyes, she will turn you into stone."

With a flick of her tail, the bird took wing and soared to the very top of the mountain. The prince watched the setting sun flash off her golden wings until she disappeared.

efore the sun rose the following morning, Prince Velimer gathered his worn blanket and what little food he had left. The jewels had long since fallen from his dagger, but the blade was still sharp. He tucked it into the top of his scuffed boot. Then he untied his horse and stroked its neck.

"The path is too steep for you, my friend. Wait for me. But if I do not return in a week, go to my father so he will know that I am dead."

The horse whinnied as Prince Velimer began to climb.

All day he scrambled over jagged rocks and fallen trees. When the moon rose, he was only one third of the way up the mountain. Shivering, he wrapped himself in his blanket and nibbled at the last of his food. As he closed his eyes to rest, he thought he heard the golden lark singing.

"Be of good cheer. I will help you if I can."

But when he opened his eyes, he saw only the stars.

The next day, the path was even more difficult to climb. Large trees gave way to stunted bushes, then to scrub. At nightfall, Prince Velimer found a small stream and he drank, but he had no food for his growling stomach. As he trembled from the cold wind that whistled through the holes in his blanket, he thought he heard the lark sing once more.

"Do not lose hope. I will help you if I can."

Before the sun had fully risen on the morning of the third day, Prince Velimer left his blanket and began to climb. Sharp stones scraped his palms and cut through his boots. Near the top of the summit, he stumbled and barely caught himself. As he clung to a large rock with trembling fingers, he heard a metallic clatter. Looking down, he saw his sharp dagger tumble over the mountainside.

Prince Velimer wanted to weep. Cold, hungry, and sore, he now had only his bare hands to battle the powerful witch. But there was no time to go after his dagger. He pulled himself up over the largest rock and crouched, looking around.

he old witch sat on a flat white stone that glistened at the very top of the mountain. Huge marble boulders curved around her like a dark cage. On her gnarled finger, the golden lark shivered.

As Prince Velimer watched, she reached out to unbind her long white hair, then stopped.

"I hear another man," the witch growled, "coming to rescue my little bird."

"It is not a man you hear," the small bird sang. "Only the souls of those who sleep, blowing over the mountain. Let your hair down and I will brush it with my wing."

Prince Velimer knelt and crept closer to the witch. He watched as she let down her heavy braid, but before she unbound it, she spoke again.

"I hear another man coming to rescue my little bird."

"It is not a man," the tiny lark trilled. "Only a poor water sprite singing in the lake below. Unbind your hair and I will fluff it with my beak."

The prince crept between two tall boulders as the old woman undid her braid. When it was almost unbound, she spoke again.

"I hear a man," the witch growled, shaking her long white hair free.

Before she finished speaking, Prince Velimer sprang forward and grabbed the witch's hair. She screamed so loudly, the mountain shook. Huge stones crashed to the valley below. Prince Velimer held tight as the old witch twisted about, kicking over heavy boulders with her large feet.

"Release me!" she finally shouted. "Release me. I will grant whatever you wish."

"I will release you when you free the little bird, and the men whom you have bewitched."

The witch tossed the bird away and opened her mouth wide. From deep within her chest a cloud of blue mist swirled into the air. As the mist touched each boulder, the stone crumbled into fine powder to reveal a living man.

When the last man was safe, Prince Velimer loosened his hold on the old witch's hair. She closed her mouth and spread her arms wide, and in an instant she turned into a tiny black moth and flew away.

he men wept with joy. Prince Velimer looked around, searching for the golden lark. Finally he found her hiding in the shadow of a tall rock. Gently he lifted her into the air.

"Fly free, little bird. You are safe," he whispered.

"One kiss, and then I shall fly free if you still wish it," the lark replied.

Prince Velimer kissed the bird. Blue mist filled the air as the last of the witch's spells shattered, and the golden bird was instantly transformed into a raven-haired maiden.

She laughed and spun in a circle, then grabbed the prince's hands and knelt.

"At last I am free," said the maiden. "The old witch captured me while I was hunting herbs in her forest. To punish me for trespassing, she held me here and used me to lure young men into her trap. When her cage of enchanted boulders was finished, no one could have defeated her."

The prince stared at the maiden. "Are you Princess Yevrossima?" he asked.

The girl nodded, and Prince Velimer grabbed her hand.

"I have been searching for you," he said. "Come, I will take you home."

So it was that Prince Velimer broke the spell that bound Princess Yevrossima. The old nurse rejoiced upon the princess's return. But the princess did not stay long. Within a week Princess Yevrossima and Prince Velimer were married.

No longer lonely, the prince returned to his father's lands. He sent away the three advisers, and he and Princess Yevrossima ruled happily by his father's side.

Eastern Europe

Russia

France

Croatia

Bosnia-
Herzegovina

Spain

Italy

Yugoslavia

Serbia is an ancient nation with a history of turmoil and war. Near the end of the seventh century, the first Serbian settlers came to this fertile region. For nearly 500 years they lived in separate tribes, often warring with each other. Finally, in the eleventh century, the tribes united to form the first Serbian state.

Three hundred years later, independent Serbia was conquered by the Ottoman Empire. During the 1800s, the Serbs fought to win back their freedom, but it wasn't until 1878 that they finally defeated the Ottoman rulers.

In 1918 Serbia became part of a new kingdom, which was named Yugoslavia. Seventy years later, as the Cold War ended, Yugoslavia divided into five different countries, which are now recognized by the United Nations. Serbia and Montenegro combined to form one of the new countries, still known as Yugoslavia. During the 1990s, Serbia has been at war with two of the other countries, Bosnia and Croatia, struggling to gain control of parts of those nations.

Despite their turbulent history, the Serbian people have a rich cultural identity, including an imaginative folklore that tells about such creatures as wood sprites, water spirits, and witches. Stories have been passed from parent to child down through the ages. *The Bird Maiden* is only one of many such stories kept alive by the Serbian folklore tradition.